Brownies - It's Christmas!

by
Gladys L. Adshead

with pictures by

Velma Ilsley

New York

Henry Z. Walck, Inc.

E

Adshead, Gladys L.
  Brownies - it's Christmas! With
pictures by Velma Ilsley.   Walck, 1955
  unp. illus.

  The Brownies finish decorating the
Christmas tree as a surprise for Old
Grandfather and Old Grandmother.

1. Christmas stories 2. Fairy tales
I. Illus. II. Title

This Main Entry catalog card may be reproduced without permission.

771032

Copyright 1955 by Gladys L. Adshead
© Gladys L. Adshead 1955
ISBN: 0-8098-1041-7 (hardcover)
ISBN: 0-8098-2913-4 (paperback)
Library of Congress Catalog Card Number: 62-17862
Printed in the United States of America

37

To
a little old grandmother
who was always young

"It's Christmas!
It's Christmas!"
shouted the Biggest
Brownie as he skipped
through
the
snowy
woods.

Lots of other brownies put their heads out of their hiding places under the roots of the big pine trees when they heard him.

"How do you know?" asked the brownies.
"Old Grandfather is coming through
the woods. He is going to cut down a
Christmas tree," the Biggest Brownie
replied. "Quick, quick! Hide yourselves."
The brownies quickly disappeared.

Old Grandfather's snowshoes shuffled softly over the snow. His long red scarf blew out in the winter wind,

his breath was steam, his nose was the color of a holly berry.

He found a fir tree just the size he wanted. He cut it down

with two strokes of his ax.

The brownies crept out from their
hiding places and followed Old
Grandfather. Their silent little
feet made no footprints in the snow.
Old Grandfather did not know that
the brownies were close behind
him.

The Smallest Brownie rode on

the back of one of Old Grandfather's
snowshoes. He bounced up and down
and had a merry time.

Old Grandfather had pulled
his cap snugly over his ears.
Fortunately he did not hear the
Smallest Brownie.

By and by they all came
to Old Grandfather's house.
It was a red house.
There was a white blanket
of snow tucked around
it and a snow pillow,
soft and thick, on
its roof.

Old Grandfather's
house looked cozy and snug.

All of a sudden, outside his door,
Old Grandfather shook the snow off
himself. It showered all over the
brownies close behind him. The
brownies were almost buried beneath
Old Grandfather's little snowstorm.

They scrambled
out and scurried
away quickly, so when
Old Grandmother
opened the door
there wasn't a
brownie to be seen.
"What a pretty tree," said Old
Grandmother. "Bring it right in."
The brownies crept inside the
house behind Old Grandfather. While

Old Grandmother was busy helping
Old Grandfather out of his coat,
they scurried ahead into the kitchen
where there was

a blazing fire.

They looked quickly around for a place to hide.

"There's a paper bag on the floor," the Biggest Brownie said, pointing. "Let's hide   in that."

So

the brownies scrambled inside the bag.

When Old Grandmother and Old Grandfather came into the kitchen there wasn't a brownie to be seen.

But the brownies couldn't see out of the bag. They were curious to know what was going on, so they began to pick holes in the paper. They made a very queer scratchy little sound.

"There are mice in this kitchen. You must set some traps, Old Grandfather," said Old Grandmother.

"I've seen no signs of mice," replied Old Grandfather.

"I heard some a minute ago," Old Grandmother said. "You must set some traps."

By this time the brownies were very very still. They didn't dare make a sound.

"I had better throw this paper bag away," said Old Grandmother suddenly. "There may be crumbs inside. Crumbs attract mice. I'll throw it on the fire."

How TERRIFIED the brownies were! They didn't know what to do. They couldn't get out of the bag without being seen.

The Smallest Brownie began to cry.

Quickly the Biggest Brownie put his hand over the Smallest Brownie's mouth. He was afraid that the old people might hear.

Old Grandmother stooped her creaky old bones to pick up the bag. The frightened brownies huddled together in a little heap inside it.

Just at that moment
Old Grandfather said
in a big loud voice, "How
much longer am I to
hold this tree before
you tell me where you
want it?"

Old Grandmother straightened
up in a hurry.

"Set it here in the middle of the table," she replied, and she forgot all about the paper bag.

How relieved the brownies were!

"We mustn't stay in this paper bag another minute," whispered the Biggest Brownie.

"Follow me."

Now Old Grandmother's big comfortable chair beside the fireplace had a fine deep frill around the bottom.

The Biggest Brownie held the Smallest Brownie's hand and led the other brownies to Old Grandmother's chair.

Old Grandmother and Old
Grandfather were busy setting
the tree up on
the table. They
didn't notice
the brownies
creeping
under
the
frill.

The brownies were safe and sound. Now they could peep out and watch Old Grandmother and Old Grandfather make the fir tree into a lovely shining Christmas tree.

Old Grandmother and Old Grandfather brought out all kinds of things: nuts, white popcorn, red cranberries, string, and, best of all, a can of gold paint, a can of silver paint, and a brush for each.

Old Grandmother and Old Grandfather put short strings on the nuts and threaded the popcorn and cranberries on l——ong strings.

Old Grandfather cut out a star for the top of the tree.

Then he and Old Grandmother began to paint the nuts. Some they painted silver, some they painted gold.

The brownies were getting tired of staying under the chair. They were especially tired of being so still and so quiet.

The Smallest Brownie was becoming fidgety, and the Biggest Brownie was afraid that the old people would hear the Smallest Brownie. He didn't know what to do.

Just then Old Grandmother said,
"I'm too tired to do any more."
"So am I!" exclaimed
Old Grandfather. "We
must rest our old
bones."
"Oh, dear,"
                Old Grandmother said with
                            a sigh.

"If we rest our old bones we shall NEVER finish the Christmas tree."
"We MUST rest our old bones," replied

Old Grandfather

firmly,

and

he got up, stretched, and went to his big comfortable chair beside the fire.

So Old Grandmother got up too and went to her big comfortable chair beside the fire. Of course the brownies were underneath it. Old Grandmother sat down with

a big
BUMP.

The brownies thought the chair
would break on top of them.

But it didn't.

In no time at all the old people were sound asleep. Old Grandmother's head nodded, and she made a sleepy little blowing sound. Old Grandfather slept with his hands folded on his stomach.

"Now is our chance," whispered the Biggest Brownie. "AT LAST we can get out. Come on, let's help the old people trim their Christmas tree."

"Let's!" cried the other brownies in their squeaky little voices,

and
they

hopped,
skipped, jumped
and

scampered

all about the old kitchen.

Some jumped—high
some jumped—low
some turned head-over-heels

They scrambled up onto the table.

Then some brownies
took the needles and
threaded cranberries

and popcorn
on the
l—ong
strings.

Some clambered into the tree.
They carried the silver and

gold nuts that the old people
had painted.

    Others climbed ahead
of them to tie the

strings
of the nuts
to the branches.

Other brownies painted more nuts
silver and gold. The brushes were
MUCH
   too big
      for them,

but they managed
somehow, and they
were very, very careful.

The Smallest Brownie wanted to help the old people too, so he took hold of some string for the cranberries. But he was too little to manage it. The string wound itself around him, around and around. It wound around his arms, about his middle, around his legs, and then an end of it suddenly popped over his head and tickled his nose. The Smallest Brownie was in a terrible tangle.

How the other brownies laughed. But
the Biggest Brownie quickly spun the
Smallest Brownie around like a top
and the string UNwound.

At last the
Smallest
Brownie
was
free.
"Whew!"
he said.

"Whew!"

"Here," said the Biggest Brownie to the smallest one. "You can help us here. Sit in the middle of the star while we paint the points on it."

So the Smallest Brownie sat very firm and still in the middle of the star. He felt very important. And

he was.

While all this was going on, four or five brownies carried the long strings of white popcorn and shiny red cranberries over their shoulders and up into the tree.

They clambered about the branches and hung the chains of berries and fluffy popcorn in lovely festoons from branch to branch,

up

and

down

and round-a-
bout

"Hurrah!" suddenly cried the brownies who were painting the star. "Hurrah! We've finished the star!" The brownies up in the tree looked down. Sure enough, there was the star — quite finished. Even the place where the Smallest Brownie had been sitting was shining silver.

"Now, HOW shall we get that big silver star to the very tip-top of the tree?" asked the Biggest Brownie, and he raised his brownie hat to scratch his head and think.

The Smallest Brownie watched him and scratched his EAR.

"A lot of us will carry it," said one brownie.

So they tried that, but there were too many brownies and they got in one another's way. They pulled and they pushed, they tugged and they shoved the star. The star stuck in the branches. It was neither up nor down. It was just halfway, and

THAT was no place
for a beautiful
    star.

The brownies were out of breath.
"What shall we do?" they asked.

The Biggest Brownie raised his
brownie hat again to scratch
his head and think hard.

"It is a very big star,"
he said at last. "And the
tip of the tree is little.
We cannot ALL go up to
the top. Just a few
brownies should help.

We will tie a string around the star. Only one brownie must go to the top, and then he can pull the star up by the string."

"Yes, yes," agreed the other brownies.

"I'm little and light," said the Smallest Brownie. "Let ME take the string to the top of the tree."

"Let him, let him," agreed the other brownies. So that was decided upon.

The Biggest Brownie tied the string around the Smallest Brownie's waist so that he would not get himself tangled in it again.

The Smallest Brownie clambered up and up to the very top. Then he pulled the string.

The brownies below scrambled up from branch to branch.

They lifted and pushed
and steered the star
very carefully
until at last
it was
    higher
        than
            the

highest
    branches.

It swung clear, just below the Smallest Brownie.

Now the Biggest Brownie climbed up as close as he could below the star. He reached up and pushed the star over to the Smallest Brownie.

The Smallest Brownie held it tightly, but he was not very good at tying string, so the Biggest Brownie climbed up beside him and tied the silver star to the

tip-top

of
the
tree.

"Hurrah! Hurrah!" cried all the brownies. "The Biggest Brownie and the Smallest Brownie have fixed the star at the top."

The brownies were delighted. They jiggled up

and

down

on

their

toes   and

forgot all about Old Grandmother and
Old Grandfather asleep in their chairs.
They made such a noise that Old
Grandmother and Old Grandfather
began to move — and to yawn—.
They were waking up!

   Like a flash the brownies scrambled
out of the tree, down to the floor and
out of doors.

Old Grandfather str——etched and yaw——ned. Old Grandmother str——etched and yaw——ned.

"Now," she said,

"we must finish our work."

When they looked at the Christmas tree they could hardly believe their eyes.
"Oh!" gasped Old Grandmother.

"Oh!" gasped Old Grandfather.

"Mice indeed!" said Old Grandfather. "Mice indeed! What you heard in that paper bag must have been BROWNIES, Old Grandmother."

Old Grandmother's eyes were shining. "Brownies they must have been," she said. "How glad I am that I didn't throw that bag on the fire. Bless the brownies' little hearts. Let's give THEM a surprise, Old Grandfather."

"A good idea, my dear," replied
Old Grandfather. "Come, we will find
the tiniest cranberries and little
 bits of fluffy white
popcorn just the right
size for brownies. Then
I will make a beautiful
little silver star just
like our big one and just the right
size for brownies too."

"And after supper," said Old Grandmother, "you will put on your snowshoes and your overcoat and your long red scarf and go into the woods to find a little fir tree just the right size for a brownie's Christmas tree."

The two old people settled happily to their work for the brownies. By

supper time all the little decorations
were ready.

   After supper Old Grandfather
put on his snowshoes, struggled into
his overcoat, and pulled his cap over
his ears.

Old Grandmother
wrapped his long
red scarf
   around
      his neck.

Then Old Grandfather went out into the white Christmas world. His pockets were full of the surprises he and Old Grandmother had made for the brownies.

The moon was shining full and round, so it was easy for Old Grandfather to find a little fir tree just the right size for a brownie Christmas tree.

Old Grandfather put his hands into his big coat pockets and pulled out the decorations.

Carefully Old Grandfather trimmed
the brownies' Christmas tree. Soon
it was laden with surprises. The
little star on top shone silver in the
moonlight.

Clear shone the stars and bright the moon as Old Grandfather went through the snowy woods back to Old Grandmother in the little red house.

Soon Old Grandmother and Old Grandfather were snug in bed and sound asleep, dreaming how happy the brownies would be to have a Christmas tree of their own.

Next morning it was Christmas.

Outside in the forest the brownies came out of their hiding places. The sun was shining on the new white Christmas day. It made the little Christmas tree very beautiful indeed.

The brownies saw the little fir tree. "Oh, my!" they exclaimed. "Oh, my!"

It looked like the Christmas tree in the little red house and just the right size for brownies.

They could hardly believe their eyes. "O..o..o..o" they sighed happily. "A Christmas tree for us!"

"Old Grandmother and Old Grandfather have given US a Christmas tree! It's BEAUTIFUL!" said the Smallest Brownie.

"Bless their old hearts," said the Biggest Brownie, "and a happy Christmas to Old Grandmother and Old Grandfather."

"A happy Christmas to everyone," called all the brownies joyfully, and they hopped

and they skipped

and they pranced

and they danced

around

and   around

their very own Christmas tree.

the end